The Move

PRAISE FOR *STORYSHARES*

"One of the brightest innovators and game-changers in the education industry."
– Forbes

"Your success in applying research-validated practices to promote literacy serves as a valuable model for other organizations seeking to create evidence-based literacy programs."

- Library of Congress

"We need powerful social and educational innovation, and Storyshares is breaking new ground. The organization addresses critical problems facing our students and teachers. I am excited about the strategies it brings to the collective work of making sure every student has an equal chance in life."
– Teach For America

"Around the world, this is one of the up-and-coming trailblazers changing the landscape of literacy and education."
- International Literacy Association

"It's the perfect idea. There's really nothing like this. I mean wow, this will be a wonderful experience for young people."   - Andrea Davis Pinkney, Executive Director, Scholastic

"Reading for meaning opens opportunities for a lifetime of learning. Providing emerging readers with engaging texts that are designed to offer both challenges and support for each individual will improve their lives for years to come. Storyshares is a wonderful start."
- David Rose, Co-founder of CAST & UDL

The Move

Michelle Henry

STORYSHARES

Story Share, Inc.
New York. Boston. Philadelphia.

Published in the United States by Story Share, Inc.

The characters and events in this book are fictitious. Any similarity to real persons, living or dead, is entirely coincidental.

Storyshares
Story Share, Inc.
24 N. Bryn Mawr Avenue #340
Bryn Mawr, PA 19010-3304
www.storyshares.org

Inspiring reading with a new kind of book.

Interest Level: High School
Grade Level Equivalent: 4.2

9781642615722

Book design by Storyshares

Printed in the United States of America

Storyshares Presents

1

Jana stared at the wall of her new house for what felt like hours. She held the dripping paintbrush by her side. Putting the brush to the wall would break the spell and make this move a reality.

Had they really moved again? Jana tried to be angry about it. She had even yelled at her mom. She thought it would make her feel better, but she just felt numb.

Crying seemed like a waste of time anyway. Jana knew that once her mom got an idea in her head, they would be stuck following the plan through to the end. Jana had felt like this many times before. It seemed like every time she would start to like a place or make new friends or love her new school, Mom would tell her it was time to leave again.

2

The place they lived in before had started to feel like to a real home. It was on such a pretty piece of land. A creek flowed quietly nearby, offering views that inspired everyone who saw them. The old barn that seemed creepy at first had become the perfect art studio. The first time she walked up those creaky stairs, Jana saw the cracked windows and the spider webs and didn't think it would be a good place to work on her art. She had been wrong.

The loft windows had a view of the tall oak trees outside. Jana had painted better things there than in any other place. Later, the perfect guy had kissed her under one of those oak trees on a perfect summer day just a few weeks ago.

Jana didn't want to even say his name. Now the happy memories were mixed with the sadness of having to move. He was close enough to call or text, but he would be too far to reach quickly by car (not that she had one of those). So she dared not spend too much time thinking of him. Jana was sure that he and her other friends would forget her soon anyway.

3

Jana remembered the exact moment when her mother walked silently into the barn. Jana knew what to expect before her mother spoke a word. She had seen that look before.

Jana barely heard the details about the better job and the awesome new school and how many friends she was sure to make. Her thoughts turned to that perfect guy and the perfect place that had inspired her to paint. Magic seemed to flow from her brush in that barn. She had paintings hung on all the walls. Her little "gallery" made her feel whole and happy.

When her mother had told her about the move, Jana had cried silently. Her tears dropped like the paint that dripped from her paintbrush. The bright, inspiring barn-studio now felt dark in Jana's memories.

Jana decided that maybe she would put her art on hold for now—at least while all she could think to paint was fiery dragons eating princesses that looked like her mother. She didn't want to slip into that dark place again, but she could feel it happening.

Jana's mother seemed cheerful about each move. Surely it was fake. Surely she couldn't really feel that way. Moving wasn't fun. Her mom was always the "new girl" at work, just like Jana was at school.

But her mom always tried to make it sound like packing up their lives was an adventure. She said things like "Jana, every time we move, you get new ideas to put on the canvas," or the best one yet, "Jana, you could be the female painter version of that famous author. You know the one."

4

Right now Jana wanted none of it. She felt as if she would never be inspired again.

Jana's mom bounced into the room with a smile. "I've got something fun for you to do!" She sang the word "do" with two syllables.

Instead of cheering Jana up, it made her clench her teeth and grip the paintbrush. She wasn't really angry, but she knew that the "fun" her mom talked about wasn't the same "fun" her friends were probably having without her.

Jana's thoughts drifted to the lake where her few friends usually laid around in the hot summer shade. They would tell stupid stories that made everyone snort with laughter. They would drink gallons of cold, Georgia sweet tea.

"Jana, come on!" Her mother's words interrupted her thoughts.

Her mom took the brush from Jana's hand. She handed Jana a large hammer and told her to tear down the wall.

Jana blinked a few times, unsure if this was real or part of her dream of destroying this place—this new "home."

"Tear down the wall, Jana. We'll call it cheap therapy." Her mother laughed and stepped back.

Jana swung the huge hammer and made a fist-sized hole in the wall. It felt good, calming. She was hurting the place that seemed to have stolen a little piece of her soul— maybe she could free the piece so that she could be whole again. The beating of the hammer made her feel like singing loud songs instead of the sad music she had been listening to lately.

When she stepped back a few minutes later, she was covered in dust. The newly damaged wall was torn apart. Pieces of wall lay in chunks on the floor. Jana examined a large piece of wall. For the first time in weeks, she wanted to paint something beautiful.

She would paint that old oak tree that she dreamed about and hang it near the window. Tearing up the room had caused the house to give her back what it stole: her life.

Maybe she would be okay after all.

The Move

About The Author

Michelle Henry is a wife of twenty-four years and a mother to two grown daughters (eighteen and twenty-two). She has been a special education teacher for twenty-five years. Writing has always been something she enjoyed, but she has only recently begun to pursue it in a serious manner. She has written several poems, three short stories, and is currently working on her first novel.

About The Publisher

Story Shares is a nonprofit focused on supporting the millions of teens and adults who struggle with reading by creating a new shelf in the library specifically for them. The ever-growing collection features content that is compelling and culturally relevant for teens and adults, yet still readable at a range of lower reading levels.

Story Shares generates content by engaging deeply with writers, bringing together a community to create this new kind of book. With more intriguing and approachable stories to choose from, the teens and adults who have fallen behind are improving their skills and beginning to discover the joy of reading. For more information, visit storyshares.org.

Easy to Read. Hard to Put Down.

www.ingramcontent.com/pod-product-compliance
Lightning Source LLC
Chambersburg PA
CBHW071231170626
46809CB00005BA/2040